Off you go, Spot!
Don't get lost.

Not in there, Spot.

Watch out!

What's in the hutch, Spot?

tap . . . tap . . .

tap . . . tap . . .

That's a funny noise . . .

tap...tap...tap...

tap...tap...tap...

. . . and that's a nice smell.

Are you hungry, Spot?

What have you found?

Now for a drink . . .

Poor Spot! Time to go home.

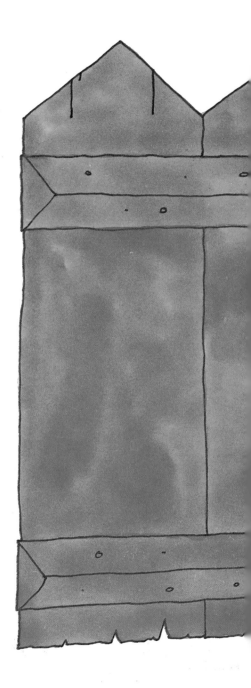